Edànì Nǫgèe Dǫne Gok'eįdì

How Fox Saved the People

Collected by Virginia Football

Illustrated by James Wedzin

Translated by Mary Siemens & Rosa Mantla

THEYTUS BOOKS

Library and Archives Canada Cataloguing in Publication

Football, Virginia
Edànì nǫgèe dǫne gok'eįdì = How the fox saved the people / collected by
Virginia Football ; illustrated by James Wedzin ; translated to English by
Mary Siemens & Rosa Mantla.

Accompanied by an audio multimedia CD in both languages.
Also issued in Dogrib and French.
Text in Dogrib and English.
ISBN 978-1-894778-75-6

1. Dogrib Indians--Folklore. 2. Foxes--Folklore. 3. Oral
tradition--Northwest Territories.
I. Siemens, Mary II. Mantla, Rosa III. Wedzin, James IV. Title.
V. Title: How the fox saved the people.

E99.D6F65 2009   398.2089'972   C2009-904383-1

Printed in China
Manufactured by Everbest Printing Co. Ltd.
Manufactured in Nansha, Guangdong, China in May 2010 Job # 403252

Yellowknife Catholic Schools

Original collected by Virginia Football
for the Department of Education, Northwest Territories
Printed in 1971 as part of a series of Tłı̨chǫ Legends

Project Coordination: Dianne Lafferty, Yellowknife Catholic Schools
Voice Recordings: Mary Rose Sundberg, Tłı̨chǫ;
Dianne Lafferty, English

Collected by: Virginia Football
Illustrated by: James Wedzin
Translated by: Mary Siemens & Rosa Mantla
Told by: Harry Mantla

THEYTUS BOOKS
www.theytus.com

Published by Theytus Books
Advising and Proofing by Anita Large
Design by Suzanne Bates
Copyediting by Julie Turner
Multimedia CD by BoggleNoggin Media Inc.

We acknowledge the financial support of the Government of Canada through the Canada Book Fund for our publishing activities.
We acknowledge the support of the Canada Council for the Arts which last year invested $20.1 million in writing and publishing throughout Canada.
Nous remercions de son soutien le Conseil des Arts du Canada, qui a investi 20,1 millions de dollars l'an dernier dans les lettres et l'édition à travers le Canada.
We acknowledge the support of the Province of British Columbia through the British Columbia Arts Council.
This publication was partially funded by the Government of the Northwest Territories.

BRITISH COLUMBIA
ARTS COUNCIL
Supported by the Province of British Columbia

 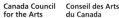
Canada Council   Conseil des Arts
for the Arts   du Canada

Canadian   Patrimoine
Heritage   canadien

Northwest
Territories Education, Culture and Employment

Introduction

For centuries the Tłįchǫ have relied on intimate knowledge of the land and wildlife, following traditional water routes and trails in the winter. We travelled towards the northeast, towards the barren land, in the fall to harvest caribou, and returned to below the treeline to winter among the caribou. In the spring and summer, rich fishing and hunting areas were occupied.

In the historic Tłįchǫ way of life, there is no written language. However, oral storytelling served as an inter-generational communication system to pass on knowledge. These stories tell of messages embedded in the landscape as place names, and that describe significant impacts and events that occurred over time.

Wherever camps were established, many stories were told over the fire. The most popular stories for all generations were about the animals and people when they spoke the same language and could understand one another. The stories were told to support and give meaning to the emotional and physical challenges of the day. The stories stirred and exercised emotion of spirit and body to help strengthen the character of the listener. The stories told were timeless and were told over and over, so that they became ingrained as part of the Tłįchǫ psyche.

A lot of the stories have fallen by the wayside in the last fifty years or so, not captured by children who were absent, away from their families in residential schools far away. There were many stories told and passed on before the Tłįchǫ moved into the modern communities, where much more reliance is placed on modern education and knowledge systems.

With the challenges of the day, voices linked to traditional stories are becoming more important with the gradual realization that our children are entitled to their ancestral based strength. We are also grateful for the stories captured and retained orally and on paper, that can be shared with the children today, so they at least will have the continued honour to exercise and pass on the traditional stories to future generations.

Dr. John B. Zoe
Executive Officer
Tłįchǫ Government

Dakwe whaà dǫne tıdeè gà nàgedè, ekwǫ̀ whìle. Dǫne wòhda edlaàtłǫ dzę ts'ǫ̀ sègeze-le. Dǫne sı bò dedì agedza.

Once upon a time, in a camp near Great Slave Lake, there were no caribou to kill. For days, the families went without food. Everyone was very hungry and weak.

Dzę taàt'e Tatsǫ̀ dǫne nàgede gots'ǫędà. Dǫne bò ghageède go nì k'eet'ı̨.
Gots'ǫędà taàt'e wı̨nà. Hanì ts'ı̨ʔǫ̀ dǫne, edànìghǫ Tatsǫ̀ wı̨nà, hagı̨ı̨wǫ.

Each day Raven landed in the camp. He would wander around looking at the hungry people. Whenever he came to the camp, he always appeared cheerful. The people were puzzled why Raven looked so happy.

Dǫne bò dę gıghadì Tatsǫ̀ ts'ǫ̀ hagedı, "Tatsǫ̀, danìghǫ negha sıgoòt'ı̨ asìı weghǫ sèts'ezè nets'ǫ?" Tatsǫ̀ hadı, "Sı̨ sı sexè łexèt'e."

The people asked Raven why he seemed so happy when they were so hungry and sad. Raven only replied, "Everything is the same with me."

Dǫne, edànìghǫ Tatsǫ̀ wegha sìgoòt'ı̨, gı̨ı̨wǫ t'à dǫne Tatsǫ̀ k'è geède ha nıxǫgı̨ʔǫ̀. Dechı̨nı wekeè kàgoı̨ʔa.

The people still wanted to know why Raven always looked so happy. They decided to follow him to see where he went. His footprints led them into the forest.

Wekeè k'è geède, hǫtsàh wekeè k'è goìle adzà. Dǫne hazǫ̀ǫ̀ k'egeet'ì̧ kò Tatsǫ̀ wexǫnàedı-le.

They followed the tracks until suddenly they came to an end.
The men looked everywhere for more signs of Raven.

Dechįnı nagıadè kò kw'ıhchįį̀ k'e k'į̀wò daèdlì gıaʔį̀. Weyìı ek'a whela nòò. "Hanì ts'ıhʔò̱ Tatsò̱ wegha sìgoòt'į nòò, bò łǫ wets'ǫ ts'ıhʔò̱. Gots'ò̱ hots'ì, ekwò̱ łǫ t'asį̀ı nàyeehʔį̀ t'ą̀ąt'e," gedı.

Suddenly, they noticed a quiver hanging on a branch of a tree.
In the quiver were pieces of frozen fat.
"No wonder Raven is so cheerful, he has lots of food.
He has lied to us," the people shouted. They thought there
must be a herd of caribou nearby.

Dǫne įłaà gogede hò, dǫne Tł'ohk'ehba wìyeh hadı, "Įdaa t'à Tatsǫ̀ wek'è dèhtła ha." Eyıt'à dǫne hazǫ̀ǫ̀ dekǫ̀ ts'ǫ̀ nageèhde. Tatsǫ̀ goghǫ noot'a gots'ǫ.

While the people were talking, a man named Tł'ohk'ehba said he would follow Raven the next time he left their camp. So, everyone returned home to wait for Raven to appear.

Satsǫ k'atsį, Tatsǫ̀ dǫne gots'ǫhtła. Dǫne łexè yatı gehtsį, Tatsǫ̀ yek'èezǫ-le. Tatsǫ̀ dǫne gıtł'ǫhbà goyìı k'eet'į̀, yeghǫ shètįį ha welìı sı gha k'eeta.

Raven visited the camp again the next day. He didn't know about the plan the people had. As usual, he entered each tent, looking for a possible meal.

Tatsǫ̀ dekǫ̀ ts'ǫ̀ naàhtła ekò k'oòhdzǫ Tł'ohk'ehba ts'ı k'e dekııtła nòò,
Tatsǫ̀ k'è k'eet'ı̨ ha t'à. Hǫtsą̀h Tł'ohk'ehba whezeh, hadı, "Asìı eehʔı̨."

Finally Raven decided to leave. Already Tł'ohk'ehba had
climbed an old spruce tree to watch him. As Raven flew away,
Tł'ohk'ehba shouted what he saw.

Tatsǫ̀ gǫwà naàht'o ts'ǫʔǫ̀ Tł'ohk'ehba yık'è gǫwà k'eet'į̀ ha dìì. Tatsǫ̀ wègaat'į adzà. Tł'ohk'ehba Tatsǫ̀ senahʔį̀ t'a ne nį̀wǫ̀.

As Raven flew farther and farther, Tł'ohk'ehba tried to follow him with his eyes, but Raven was flying out of sight. Tł'ohk'ehba was worried he might lose Raven.

Tł'ohk'ehba hadı, "Łèbè sets'abeè k'e aahdı!" Łèbè wets'abeè k'e geèhtso. Wet'à wegha nezı̨ı̨ xègaat'ı adzà. "Nezı̨ı̨ segha wègoèht'ı̨. Shìh ts'ǫ dèht'o wègaat'ı. Ekǫ ts'ǫ wek'è ts'ııdè," hadı.

Tł'ohk'ehba asked someone to wipe his forehead with ashes.

This helped him to see better.

"I can see him now," cried Tł'ohk'ehba.

"He's landing near a hill. Let's follow him there!"

Dǫne Tł'ohk'ehba k'è geède. Dechįnı nıwà geède t'à dǫne nègįįtsǫ̀ǫ̀ agedzà.

The People started walking through the forest to find Raven.
It was a long walk and everyone became very tired.

Nǫdèa shìh gà nègı̨ı̨de edı̨ı̨ Tł'ohk'ehba nǫde Tatsǫ̀ eʔı̨ı̨ sı. Tatsǫ̀ wexònaì dı-le nòò. Ts'ımòkǫ̀ nechàa gıaʔı̨. Hanì et'ıì dǫne ts'ımòkǫ̀ wemǫ̀ǫ̀ nègı̨ı̨de.

Finally they arrived at the hill where Tł'ohk'ehba had last seen Raven. At first they didn't see any sign of the bird. Then, they noticed a big spruce hut nearby. Quickly the People surrounded the hut.

Dìga gıghǫnììgè. Dìga hadı, "Naxıgha goyìı k'ııht'į̀," gòhdı.

Wolf, who happened to appear then, offered to enter the hut to see what was inside.

Dìga goyeèhgè, kǫ̀ wegodo ʔǫhchì yìı bò dàgoòʔǫ wha k'e dawhehtǫ yaʔį. ʔǫhchì nedàa neyįį̀hxè gà dǫne gots'ǫ̀ bò kàyeèxè.

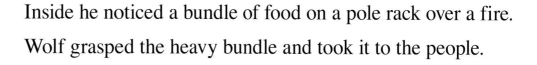

Inside he noticed a bundle of food on a pole rack over a fire.
Wolf grasped the heavy bundle and took it to the people.

Dǫne hazǫ̀ǫ̀ gı̨nà, sègeze ha ts'ǫʔǫ̀. Tatsǫ̀ edı̨̀ı̨ ts'ǫ bò ayehʔı̨ dǫne hagı̨ı̨wǫ, gıgòhʔa ha gı̨ı̨wǫ, ı̨daa t'à k'atsı̨ sègeze ha t'à. Dǫne hagedı, "Amìı goyaetła gà gogha Tatsǫ̀ k'e nàeʔı̨̀ ha?" gedı. Nogèe goghǫnı̨̀ı̨hgè, hadı.

Everyone was happy to have food to eat. However, they decided to find out where Raven was getting his food, so they would have meat for their next meal. "Who will enter the hut to spy on Raven?" the crowd asked. This time Fox offered to help.

"Chekoa wha k'e dagìahwha, naxį dǫne įdè nàahza!" hadı.

Fox told the people to put all the children on a pole rack so they would be safe. The adults stood nearby to watch.

Dǫne ts'atà nègįįde tł'àxǫǫ Nǫgèe ts'ımòkǫ̀ goyeèhgè, detsè kǫ̀ nì kw'įyįgeh. Wetsè dehsho ts'ǫʔǫ̀ ło łǫ agòdzà.

When People were ready, Fox entered the hut. Once inside, he brushed the fire with his bushy tail. This made large clouds of smoke.

Hanì et'ıì nǫgèe kàgee, wek'è łǫ nııt'ıı ladzà. Dǫ ts'ehwhį̀ nageèh?į̀.

Quickly Fox trotted outside, with a trail of smoke following him. Everyone waited patiently.

Hǫtsǫ̀h eezıı xèleekw'ǫ̀ lagòdzà. Ts'ımòkǫ̀ gots'ǫ ekwǫ̀ łǫ kàjıgogeèhwho.
Ekwǫ̀ goxa naeʔàa sı dǫne k'ı̨̀ t'à gogıhtà.

Soon there was a loud noise which sounded like thunder.

Suddenly a large herd of caribou ran from the spruce hut.

The hunters began spearing the caribou as they ran past.

Ekwò ełagehde ghǫ nagııt'e tł'axǫǫ Tatsǫ̀ wııts'ǫą tàatǫǫ eyıts'ǫ wechoò dè k'e k'eagot'o nòò, eyıt'à ts'ǫ̀ǫkoa etse. Ts'ǫ̀ǫkoa hadı, "Tatsǫ̀ weladì? Tatsǫ̀ wınì gǫǫzǫ̀ǫ t'à gogha wet'àaʔaa ıłè."

When they were finished, the people noticed a pair of crumpled wings and bits of feather on the ground. An Old Woman started to cry when she saw this.
"Where is Raven? We need the wise Raven!" she cried.

Ts'o̧o̧koa, Tatso̧ wı̧ts'o̧a̧ eyıts'o̧ wechoò k'eagot'o sı hazo̧o̧ nàyehtsı, to degà nèyı̧ı̧wa gà dètı̧.

The woman picked up the pieces of bone and feather and put them beside her when she went to sleep at night.

K'emoòdǫ̀ǫ̀ ts'ǫ̀ǫ̀koa ts'ı̨ı̨wo Tatsǫ̀ godì wegà whetì nǫ̀ǫ̀, t'à sı wı̨nà. Tatsǫ̀ dǫne gots'ǫ̀ nezı̨ı̨̀ eghàlaı̨dà-le yek'eelı̨. Nǫgèe yenahk'e gǫǫzǫ̀ǫ̀ k'ehoʔa t'à dǫne gok'eı̨dì yek'èezǫ.

The next morning, she found a live Raven sleeping beside her. The Old Woman was very happy to see that Raven was not dead. Raven felt sorry that he had hidden the caribou. He knew that Fox had outwitted him, and had saved the People from starving.

The Dogrib Language and Its Family[1]

The Dogrib language belongs to a close family of about thirty languages. In this Na-Dene or Athapaskan family of languages, Slave and Chipewyan are the most similar to Dogrib. Because of the similarities among the languages, some Dogrib people can understand Slave or Chipewyan.

Languages related to Dogrib are spoken in the western Northwest Territories, northern parts of Manitoba, Saskatchewan, Alberta, and British Columbia, the Yukon Territory, and Alaska. More Na-Dene languages are or were spoken in western parts of Washington, Oregon, and California. In the dry desert plateaus of Colorado, New Mexico, and Arizona, and in some areas of northern Mexico, the southern relatives of the Dogrib language, Apache and Navajo, are spoken.

All of the people who originally spoke Na-Dene languages come from one people, and the Na-Dene languages were once one language. As time passed, and people moved and migrated, the language gradually changed so that people living in different areas now speak their own distinctive Na-Dene languages. The process of change continues today but the shared heritage of the languages means that many words are similar.

Just as languages change as they migrate across countries, over time, different regions take on their own dialects because of isolation or exposure to other language groups. While most words remain the same among dialects, some pronunciations may shift or change depending on the affecting influence. Each of the communities in which Dogrib is spoken has its own dialect uniqueness.

[1] The Dogrib language and Its Family information can be found in Leslie Saxon and Mary Siemens, eds. *Tłįchǫ Yatìì Enįhtł'è*: A Dogrib Dictionary (Dogrib Divisional Board of Education 1992).

Dogrib Orthography and Pronunciations

Dene Font - The Dogrib language is written using the Dene font. You will notice that the letter "i" is not dotted in this font. This is to avoid confusion with the low tone markings used in the Dogrib language "ì".

Dogrib Alphabet - There are forty-one letters in the Dogrib alphabet. It has four "plain vowels" (a e i o) which can change through nasal and tonal markings, resulting in sixteen different ways to express vowel sounds:

Plain Vowels - the air, which makes the sound of these vowels, flows through the mouth like vowels in English, e.g., ı as in dı, this sounds like the i in the word sk**i**.

Nasal Vowels - the air flows through the nose and the mouth, e.g., ı̨ as in dı̨ sounds like the e in the word m**ea**n.

Low Tone Plain Vowels - the air flows through the mouth, and the tone is held a little bit longer with a low voice e.g., ìe as in dìe sounds like dee in English but it is held longer.

Low Tone Nasal Vowels - the air flows through the nose and the mouth, and the tone is held a little bit longer with a low voice e.g., į̀ as in dį̀į̀ (four times), sounds like "mean" but the vowel sound is held a little longer.

You can listen to the sounds of the above vowels, letters and words on your computer with the attached multimedia CD or if you do not have a computer you can place the CD into your CD player to follow along.

The following chart lists all of the Dogrib letters, and provides Dogrib words that illustrate the sound of the letters and shows the closest English equivalent to the Dogrib sound.

Dogrıb Orthography and Pronuncıatıons

Letter	Dogrib Word	English Translation	Closest English Sound
ʔ	ʔah tł'àʔeh	snowshoe pants	the 'click' sound which we hear in the expression "oh-oh"
a	amà ladà	mother table	father; when **a** is nasalized (ą), it is similar to the sound in w<u>an</u>t
b	bebì k'ehbe	baby I am swimming	<u>b</u>a<u>b</u>y
ch	chǫ nechà	rain it is big	<u>ch</u>; some people pronounce this sound more like what we hear in wet<u>s</u>uit
ch'	ch'oh sech'à	quill against me	the same as **ch**, but with the 'click' sound as part of it
d	done nedè	person your younger sister	<u>d</u>id
dl	dlìą nàʔets'edlò	mouse we are laughing	ba<u>dl</u>y; or sometimes like g<u>l</u>ue
dz	dzèh edza	spruce gum cold weather	a<u>dz</u>e
e	ehtł'è wetà hęʔę	mud, dirt his or her father yes	s<u>e</u>t; when e is nasalized, it is similar to the sound in s<u>en</u>t; in a prefix after w, it is similar to w<u>oo</u>d
g	gah nàhgą gomǫ	rabbit bushman our mother	<u>g</u>o
gh	segha weghàts'eeda	for me we are looking at it	no similar sound in English; similar to the <u>r</u> sound in the French *rouge* "red"
gw	ehgwàa	dryfish	lang<u>ua</u>ge
h	hanì ehtsèe	in this way grandfather	<u>h</u>at; in Dogrib this sound can be pronounced inside or at the end of a word
ı	lıdì mı̨̀ yeht'ì	tea fish net she or he is pulling it	sk<u>i</u>; when ı is nasalized, it is similar to the sound in m<u>ea</u>ns

t	**t**ı netà	water your father	<u>t</u>en
t'	**t'**eeko **t'**o	young woman paddle	the same as t, but with the "click" sound as part of it
tł	**tł**į danet**ł**o	dog dance	se<u>ttle</u>; or sometimes more like <u>cl</u>ue
tł'	**tł'**ı enįh**tł'**è	rope paper, book	the same as **tł**, but with the "click" sound as part of it
ts	**ts**o eh**ts**į	firewood granny	ca<u>ts</u>
ts'	**ts'**ah **ts'**ǫ̀ko	hat old woman	the same as ts, but with the "click" sound as part of it
w	**w**età lıdì**w**ò	his or her father teabag	<u>w</u>et; in a prefix, w with a following e sounds similar to <u>woo</u>d
wh	**wh**a lıdì de**wh**ǫ **wh**ǫ	marten I want tea star	breathy <u>wh</u> as in <u>wh</u>en; in a prefix, wh with a following e sounds like <u>whir</u>r.
x	**x**ah go**x**è **x**ok'e	goose with us winter	no similar sound in English; a raspy h, similar to the German <u>ch</u> as in *Bach* (the composer)
y	**y**ahtı k'e**y**ege kw'à**y**ìą	priest carrying bowl	<u>y</u>et
z	**z**ǫ de**z**ǫ lı**z**à whe**z**ò	only it is black ace (in cards) it is crooked	<u>z</u>oo
zh	**zh**aka goh**zh**ì goį**zh**ǫ į**zh**ìı	the top of the snow shadows he or she is smart down	plea<u>s</u>ure; some people pronounce this sound more like what we hear in plea<u>s</u>e

j	jɪe jǫ dejɪ̨	berry here she or he is scared	jet; some people pronounce this sound more like what we hear in a<u>dz</u>e
k	ke ts'èko	footwear woman	<u>k</u>it; in prefixes, it is sometimes pronounced like **x** or **h**
k'	k'àle ek'ı̨̀	spider fish eggs	the same as **k**, but with the "click" sound as part of it
kw	kwe ekwǫ̀	rock caribou	<u>qu</u>it
kw'	kw'ah ekw'ǫ̀ǫ̀	moss bones	the same as kw, but with the "click" sound as part of it
l	lɪdì elà	tea canoe	<u>l</u>et
ł	łǫ ełexè	many together	breathy <u>l</u>; similar to the <u>l</u> in f<u>l</u>ip or s<u>l</u>ip
m	mı̨̀ masì	fish net thank you	<u>m</u>et
mb	nambè **mb**ò **mb**eh	summer meat knife	ru<u>mb</u>le; many people use the b sound instead of **mb**
n	nezɪ̨ gonè	it is good our land	<u>n</u>et; sometimes **n** is contracted with a vowel to make a nasalized vowel
nd	sı̨**nd**e **nd**ɪ	my older brother island	sa<u>nd</u>al; many people use the **d** sound instead of **nd**
o	ło det'ǫcho whek'**ò**	smoke eagle it is cold	g<u>o</u>; some people pronounce this sound more like g<u>oo</u>; when o is nasalized, it is similar to the sound in d<u>on</u>'t
r	ʔorɪ	spruce bough	similar to ca<u>rr</u>y; some people almost never use this sound and just leave it out
s	sa sechɪa	month, sun my little brother	<u>s</u>et

Source: Leslie Saxon and Mary Siemens, eds. *Tłı̨chǫ Yatıì Eną̀htł'è: A Dogrib Dictionary*. Dogrib Divisional Board of Education, 1992.

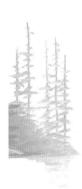

Dànì Nogèe Dǫ K'eı̨dì

How the Fox Saved the People

Told by Harry Mantla, Tłı̨chǫ Elder

Dǫ nàdè ts'edı, dǫ łǫǫ nàdè ts'edı. Dǫ łǫ nàdèe sìı nàgezè, nàgezè. Dzę taàt'eè ts'otanagedè, ts'otanagedè, ekìanì, dǫ nàdè, dǫ nàdè. Dàòdì asìı ełagehwhı-le, bò whìle hodeèwo. Bò whìle hodeèwo t'à chekaa hanıı sìı bòdę yàgıdlı ha wolì lanı bòdę hodeèwo. Hòt'a dzę taàt'e lanì ts'otanagedè hò asìı wıızìı ełagehwhı-le, dàòdì. Dàòdì, dzę taàt'e lanì aget'į.

Nìlàà-hį̀į̀ Satsǫ dǫ ghaèhtła ts'edı. T'à k'et'a ne ts'eʔǫ ı̨doe tso agehʔı̨ı̨ sìı ekǫ t'aa dèhtła sǫnıà, eyıts'ǫ dǫ ts'ǫ èhtła, ʔah yìeta gà. K'ızòa hanıı tehmì k'egee sìı edaà hanıı yeghǫ sètı̨ ha nıwǫ hìı hanıı nàke dechı̨a weghaı̨ʔa gà tehmì yìı yèhła, hanì t'à deghàyeèchì sǫnıà. Hanì t'aa dǫ ts'ǫ èhtła, dǫ ghǫ nìıtła.

Dìga sìı weye ne ts'edı. T'à Dìga sìı, "Seye-e-e holǫǫ at'į hı̨ı̨là. Seye nìıtła nǫǫ," dìı t'aa, "Dzǫ hòt'a chekaa bòk'edeèhdlı. Nı̨ t'a whaèhdǫǫ̀ laànı anet'e, nı̨ t'à asìı hazǫǫ̀ k'èı̨zǫ sǫnaà. Dzǫ hòt'a, dzę taàt'e nats'ezè, whı̨ats'et'ı̨ hòt'a chekaa goghǫ bòk'edeèhdlı," yèhdı ts'edı.

Į̀lèe-hį̀į̀, "Hazǫǫ̀ ełègode, ełègode, ełègode," dìı t'a deye Dìga xègoèhdo ts'edı. Hòt'a, dzęghàà łegà gıakw'è, łexè gogedo, łexè gogedo, łexè gogedo. Hòt'a xèhts'ǫ agòdzàa-t'a, "Sekǫ̀ gǫǫwà t'à hòt'a naehtła ha," hadı ts'edı. "Hòt'a naehtła ha," hadı ts'edıà.

Į̀laà naetła kwe-t'ìı nàgoʔı̨a t'à," Į̀doe ts'ǫ nììtła sìı wekeè k'è goghàahda ahxǫ asìa deda nèechì hǫt'e lì, gedı t'à wenaàhtǫa t'a dǫ ekǫǫ̀ geède, chekaa ekǫ geède. Į̀làa, tehmìa deghàèchì nǫǫ eyı dèht'o ts'ǫ, tehmìa deghàèchì nǫǫ gıyìk'eeta, į̀lè-hį̀į̀ edaàlıa nàke weghachı̨eʔa weyìı whela. Wenaàhtǫa hazǫǫ̀ hałègeedı, "Edaà nàke tehmì yìwhehłah kò adı nǫǫ̀," gedı.

Hòt'a xèhts'ǫ ne ts'ıhʔǫ naehtła ha hadı. Hòt'a naèhtła. Eyıt'à, amèe dìıle sìı ı̨k'ǫǫ̀ t'à weèdzà ha ts'oʔǫ yeè hazǫǫ̀ kǫ̀ta nàłegıızah, gedıà. Naèhtła tł'axǫǫ̀ t'aa edaàlıa hanıı nàke tehmì yìı whehłaa sìı "Ekìadı nǫǫ̀, ekwǫ̀ ts'ǫ at'ı̨ kò adı ne," gedıà t'à nıdahogı̨į̀hdè, e-e-ełetahàkwıgı̨į̀de.

Tł'ok'ehbaa gedıı sìı, "Sı̨ dè dìıle, sı̨ dè dìı-le," dıà. Hòt'a naèht'o tł'axǫǫ̀ ı̨k'ǫǫ̀ t'à yek'è k'eet'ı̨. Yek'è k'eet'ı̨ t'à yee hanì, hanì yek'edaehta, t'a ekǫ nat'a, nat'a, dı gedià. Dagǫǫwà naèht'o daats'ǫ̀, "Hòt'a segha wègaat'ı̨-le adaade. Gǫǫwà naèt'ǫ dìı, hòt'a segha wègaat'ı̨-le daade," dı.

Į̀làa dıı kǫ̀èk'ǫ ne-àlı, "Łèbè hanıı senazı aahtsı, łèbè hìı senazı aahtsı," goèhdı t'à hagı̨į̀là, ts'edıà. Łèbè gınazıèhtsoò t'à, "Nezı̨į̀ wènagoèht'ı̨," dı, gedıà. Nezı̨į̀ wènagoèht'į̀į̀ t'àlìı , hotìı nezı̨į̀ waı̨daà, wek'enaı̨hta, gìıhdı. Yek'e naehta, yek'e naehta, hòt'a, "Shìh lanıı teèht'ǫ, hòt'a ı̨zhıì shìh te ts'ǫ, ı̨zhıì ts'ǫèlè," dı. "Eyı hòt'a sìıh te ts'ǫ, hòt'a eyı ts'ǫ zǫ k'è hoòle, dı, gedıà.

Hatsǫ hots'eèhdzà ha ne ts'ǫʔǫ̀ dǫ sìı ekǫ ts'eedè ha. Weye Dìga, sìı k'àowo ne hǫnaà, eyı dǫ nàdè gha sìı. Hatsǫ hazǫǫ̀ ts'eedè ha ne ts'eʔǫ hazǫǫ̀ k'emeèdǫ et'ìı ts'eedè ha," dìı t'a gotaà ezeh.

Į̀làa k'emeèdǫ t'a hazǫǫ̀ dǫ dède, edı̨į̀ ts'ǫ sìı ekǫ dǫ dède ts'edı. Gıadè, gıadè, gıadè, gǫǫwà ne sǫnı hò hanì hòt'a ekǫ dǫ dède. Gıadè, gıadè, hotìı eyı ne nı̨wò ı̨lèe sìı ekǫ nègı̨ı̨deè.

Įlèè-hįį eyi nàdee sìi gıts'ǫedè, ts'edìà. Gıts'ǫede hòt'a, įlèè daht'o nàk'e k'e hotìi bò dagoòɂǫ ts'edı, daht'ǫ nàk'e k'e bò dawhela nǫǫ.

Įlèè-hįį Dìga dakwełǫǫ etłe ne t'à-alìi , Dìga sìi daht'o hodàdeèdo ts'edìà, įłè hodàyeèdo t'à k'achį įłè anayììdlà, k'achį ıłè hodàyerèdo. "Seye bò whìle nįdı, bò whìle nįdı, ełègode, ełègode, ełègode, nįdı là, seweèk'enıwheɂà ne nǫǫ," dìà t'à daht'o hodàdeedee ts'edìà. Hanìkò dǫ ts'ǫ xàetła-le ts'edı, Hatsǫ̀.

Hòt'a daht'o hodàdeèdoo sìi gınaɂǫ̀ hazǫǫ̀ nàgedè nèhogįįɂǫ. Eyı bò hò hazǫǫ̀ dǫ taɂedì, dǫ taɂedì, dǫ taɂedì, hotìi ełètłǫ dǫ taɂedì, hòt'a bò ghǫ shègeze, k'ǫat'a hǫzįį hoògǫa agòdzà.

Įlèè, k'achį bòk'enahodeèhwo, bò k'e nahodeèhwoò hòt'à k'achį dàgǫ̀ht'e įlèe sìi k'achį hanagòdzà. K'achį hanagòhdzà hòt'a k'achį nałegìkǫ ts'edı.

Nałegìkǫ įlèè-sįį eyı nàdee sìi ekwǫ̀ goyınııhɂà t'à ekwǫ̀ ts'ǫda kǫ̀ nègonìįhɂǫ nǫǫ̀ ts'edı. Ekwǫ̀ ts'ǫda kǫ̀ nègonìįhɂǫ nǫǫ̀ t'à k'achį įk'ǫǫ̀ t'à nałegìkǫ. Hatsǫ̀ sìi ekwǫ̀ goyınııhɂà t'à ekwǫ̀ sìi hazǫǫ̀ yets'ǫda nìkǫ̀nènııhɂǫ nǫǫ̀ ts'edı. K'achį yegha nałegìkǫ ts'edı.

Eyıt'à, "Amèe ayį̀įlà –elì? Amèe ayį̀įlà įdè?" gedìı t'à hazǫǫ̀ ełegìkǫ,

ts'edı. Įlèè-hįį Nomba sìi hadı ts'edı, "Sį dè dìı-le sǫnı," dı ts'edìà. "Įt'à nį dìı-le dè įwhąą wenìnįįhdzà. K'achį t'agǫ̀ht'e sìi hanagòhdzà. Bò whìle anagòdzà lìı, nį dìı-le dè wenìįhdzà," nageedı gedìà. "Heɂę sį dè dìı-le," dı, ts'edìà. It'aa, "Įda kǫ̀èk'ǫ ne ts'eɂǫ nį dìı-le dè wenìįhdzà ha t'į̀t'e ne –àlı," hagıìhdı ts'edı.

Hanì-at'a, įda kǫ̀dèk'ǫ ts'eɂǫ Nomba sìi t'a edetsè kwıìłanıhtł'a ts'edìà, t'a hanì-et'ìı xàèhts'ì ts'edìà. Xàèhts'ì t'à yekǫ̀ sìi goyaèhts'ì, hanìet'ìı t'a edį̀į ekwǫ̀ goyınııhɂà įlèe sìį ekwǫ̀ tǫts'ì hǫnaà, Eı-ı-ı ekwǫ̀ ta naèts'ì t'a hanì-at'a ekwǫ̀ eki xàłeèhzah ts'edı. Ekwǫ̀ xàłeèhzah t'à eki, "Dì-ı-ı-ì," goòdzà t'a ekwǫ̀ xàłeèhzah.

Įlèè-hįį Hatsǫ̀ sìi ekwǫ̀ goyınııhɂàa įlèe sįį eki wetsoa zǫ k'eagòt'ǫ ts'edı, wetsoa zǫ k'eagòt'ò ts'edı. Eyı tł'axǫǫ̀ t'a ekwǫ̀ łǫ agòdzà. Įlèè-hįį Hatsǫ̀ wetsoa zǫ k'eagòt'ǫ-àlı, Dìga sìı hanì ha dìì, hanì ha dìì nıwǫ, t'sedı. Hanì ha dìì-àlı, hanì ha dìì ts'eɂǫ, yedanıwo ts'eɂǫ, hanì seye weahdì ha dìì nıwǫ, ts'edı. Dìga sìı yet'aà gwìa-a nàwhehtsį ts'edı. Yet'aà łąą nèyįįwa t'à nılèè Satsǫ̀ nahdlį ts'edı.

Satsǫ̀ nahdlįį hòt'a "Ełègode, ełègode nįdı-à seweèk'enıwheèɂa ıłè nǫǫ̀," hayèhdı ts'edı. Eyıt'à dǫ

nelį gots'ǫ asìı wızìı ełaįhwhı ha-le. Dıınèe nàąwo gots'ǫ tłįtsǫ nekwį zǫ t'à įda ha ne." Dìga deye haèhdı, ts'edı. Eyıts'ıhɂǫ̀ dıı dzęę k'e ts'ǫ Dìga sìı hayèhdı ts'edıı sìı Satsǫ̀ dıı dzęę k'e ts'ǫ hanì hǫt'e.

Eyıt'à nàts'edè dè tłį daetł'į̀į dè tłį tł'axǫǫ̀ dè k'eɂehkà, k'eɂehkaà. Hòt'a Dìga hayèhdıı sìı eyı k'è edaà adzà hǫt'e, Satsǫ̀.

To keep the integrity of the story as Harry so graciously told it, we present a near-literal translation. It preserves the animated and circular nature of oral storytelling, including the additional explanations and repetitions that an Elder would use to tell a story. For Harry, and for all storytellers, legends are tools for teaching.

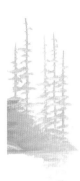

How Fox Saved the People

Told by Harry Mantla
Tłı̨chǫ Elder

It was said that people were living in camps. It was a big camp of many people. The people hunted and hunted. Every day they would go to the bush. Going to the bush; people just lived that way. Nothing. They didn't kill anything. Starvation was setting in. It seemed like the children were going to starve, as starvation was setting in. Even though the people went into the bush every day they didn't kill a thing, nothing. Nothing, they went like that every day.

At that time it was said that Raven came upon some people. Because he was flying, he landed where the people were collecting firewood, I suppose. He put on his snowshoes and went to meet the people. The birchbark sack he was carrying had two caribou eyes skewered with small sticks that he wanted to snack on later. In that way, I suppose, he hung up his birchbark sack on a tree branch. Having done that, he met up with the people.

It was said that Wolf was his brother-in-law. So Wolf, upon seeing Raven, said, "My brother-in-law usually travels far and wide! My brother-in-law has come to visit us!" he said, "The children here are starving. You are like an old-timer; you must know a lot of things. We have been hunting every day without success, but the children are starving in front of us." This is what he said to him. Raven, it was said, told his brother-in-law, "We are all in the same situation, all in the same situation, all in the same situation." They spent the whole day together, telling each other story after story. Finally evening came. Raven said, "Because my home is so far away I am going home now; I am leaving now."

Just before Raven left to get his sack in the bush they said, "Look for his tracks. Follow his tracks from where he came from in the bush. Maybe he left something for himself." The young men went there without his knowledge. Just then, they saw the sack he had hung up from the time he landed. They began to search the sack and found to their surprise two frozen caribou eyeballs. They said to each other without his knowledge, "He spoke that he was starving even though he kept two caribou eyes in his sack."

Because it was evening Raven said he was leaving. "I'm leaving now." So he left.

It was said that the whole village was searched for whoever might have medicine power to help. After Raven left, the two frozen caribou eyeballs he had in his sack were discussed. "He spoke even though he came from where the caribou were," they argued.

The one they call Tł'ohk'ehbaa said, "If it was me I can do it," he said. After Raven flew away, Tł'ohk'ehbaa followed him by using his medicine power. He followed him, on and on, for a long distance spying on him, by flying, flying there, they said.

After Raven flew high, "I can't see him anymore. He is flying too high, I'm losing him," Tł'ohk'ehbaa said. There was fire burning in the firepit, so he said, "Smear ashes across my eyelids, smear ashes across my eyelids." It was said they did that to him.

As they smeared the ashes across his eyelids, Tł'ohk'ehbaa said, "He is reappearing clearly." Because he could clearly see him again, they told him to take a good look at Raven and spy on him. He spied and spied on him. Finally he said, "He flew over something like a mountain, over and down the mountain, he's gone down there. It's over the mountain, it's the only place he went to," he said.

"Tomorrow we are going to investigate it so we will go there with the people," said Wolf. It is said that as the brother-in-law, Wolf was in charge of the people living there.

"Because we are all leaving tomorrow we will all leave early," said the Wolf among the people.

Everybody left in the morning, it was said. People went to where Tł'ohk'ehbaa had seen Raven go. They walked and walked and walked. It may have been far. I don't know if the people slept, but the people were on their way to that area. They walked and walked and finally they arrived at the very spot that Tł'ohk'ehbaa thought it was.

Then those living in the area came out to meet them. It was said that as they came out the people saw two drying racks full of meat. They were surprised to see meat hanging on the two drying racks. Suddenly, because the Wolf was ahead of the people, it was said that he pushed down the drying racks. He pushed down one and he did the same to the other one. "My brother-in-law, you said there was no meat, no meat; you said we are all in the same situation, same situation; isn't that what you said? You were risking my life," he said. It was said that he threw down the drying racks, but Raven never came out to him.

The people began to live next to the heap of drying racks and meat. They shared all that meat among the people.

They shared and shared equally among themselves. They ate the meat and just when things were beginning to improve, the meat was all used up. The meat was all eaten up, so that what the situation was like at the beginning happened again. (They were all starving again.)

Since it happened again it is said that they began to search out each other's medicine power. As they searched out each other's medicine power it is said that someone was living there. The caribou had gone into an enclosure. They were trapped at the entrance by someone's house. The caribou were trapped in there. It was said that Raven had his house at the entrance to trap in all the caribou.

It was said that the people started to search each other's power. So, it was said that they asked, "Who will do it, who would it be?" They asked as they searched each other's medicine power. To their surprise Fox said, "I might be able to do it." So, they said, "If you are able to do it, try it. The situation is starting all over again. There is no more meat. If you can do it then try it."

"Yes, if it is me I can do it. "he said. So they said to him, "There is fire in the firepit, if you are able to you will try it." So since there was fire in the firepit it was said that Fox flung his tail in the firepit and immediately ran out. He ran into Raven's house and immediately ran among

the caribou that were in there. "E-i-i-I!" he yelled as he ran among the caribou. In that moment, it is said, the caribou began to rush out. As the caribou rushed out their hooves thundered like, "Dì-i-i-ì."

All that was left of Raven who was among the trapped caribou were his few feathers scattered around. It was said, only his few feathers were scattered around. After that there was a lot of caribou.

Because Raven's feathers were scattered all over Wolf thought it was not right. It was said he thought it should not be that way. It was said that he thought about it and he couldn't leave his brother-in-law like that. It was said that Wolf gathered his bits of feather and put it in a pile. Suddenly he became Raven again, it is said.

When Raven became alive, Wolf said, "When you said, we are all in the same situation, you were putting my life in danger," he said to him. As long as you are a person you will never kill anything. As long as you live on this earth you will live only by pecking at dog feces," Wolf said to his brother-in-law, it was said. That is why to this day what Wolf said to Raven is that way to this day.

So when we live in camps, he hops and pecks around places where dogs have been. In the end, Raven lives according to what Wolf said to him.

Cultural Education Benefitting Children and Youth

First Nations peoples have passed on traditional knowledge through the generations through oral storytelling and traditional practices. In many First Nations communities, the Nation owns the communities' legends and knowledge. Storytellers tell their version of the story, yet they always maintain the integrity of the events and messages within that story. For this reason, we have included the original recording of this story as told by a Tłįchǫ Elder. We continue to make efforts to maintain the integrity of each legend even as we change its form from the original oral tradition to the written word.

Many storytellers acknowledge and respect the communal ownership of the legends. As such, these Tłįchǫ books are copyrighted to the Tłįchǫ Nation. Yellowknife Catholic Schools and Theytus Books have given all royalties back to the community. At the request of the Tłįchǫ Nation, the Aboriginal Special Collection of the Tłįchǫ Nation's Chief Jimmy Bruneau School benefits from the sale of the book to encourage the traditional practice of passing knowledge through stories. Says Dr. John B. Zoe, "Our intention is to build a comprehensive library of our legends and other cultural stories here for the use of our children and youth."

Editorial Note

Theytus Books would like to acknowledge the respectful approach that Dianne Lafferty has taken in ensuring that all cultural protocols were followed in making this work a reality. Dianne has consulted with Theytus Books and has ensured that all cultural permissions were granted. This story was respectfully edited in line with Theytus' cultural protocols and the teachings of the Tłįchǫ Nation and its Elders.